THE CHRISTMAS MOUSE

BY ELISABETH WENNING

DRAWINGS BY BARBARA REMINGTON

HOLT, RINEHART AND WINSTON

NEW YORK

Published by Holt, Rinehart and Winston,
383 Madison Avenue, New York, New York 10017.

Published simultaneously in Canada by Holt, Rinehart
and Winston of Canada, Limited.

Library of Congress Cataloging in Publication Data

Wenning, Elisabeth.
    The Christmas mouse.

    Summary: A little mouse living in the church of an
Austrian village assuages his hunger by feasting on
the organ bellows and causing the priest and the
organist to quickly compose a song for Christmas Eve
Mass, the now famous "Silent Night, Holy Night."
    1. Gruber, Franz Xaver, 1787–1863—Juvenile fiction.
2. Mohr, Joseph, 1792–1848—Juvenile fiction.
[1. Mice—Fiction. 2. Gruber, Franz Xaver, 1787–1863—
Fiction. 3. Mohr, Joseph, 1792–1848—Fiction.
4. Christmas—Fiction. 5. Austria—Fiction]
I. Remington, Barbara, ill. II. Title.
PZ7.W46923Ch 1983   [E]   83-12660

ISBN 0-03-015066-3

Printed in the United States of America
20 19 18 17 16 15 14 13 12

ISBN 0-03-015066-3

TO THOSE WHO
TAUGHT ME
'SILENT NIGHT'—
MY FATHER
AND MOTHER
          E.W.

ONCE UPON A TIME long, long ago there lived a little mouse in the village of Oberndorf near Salzburg, Austria. His name was Kaspar Kleinmaus—Kaspar Little Mouse.

Although he was the tiniest creature in the whole town, he had the biggest house, the Church of St. Nicholas. But he never felt lonely because it was his home. He had been there since the day he was born.

When he was all by himself in the church he liked to sit and think about the time that he had first been discovered and given a name. Kaspar would never forget that night.

He had wanted to sniff some fir trees newly placed around the side altar. So, up he went.

Kaspar was so surprised. There in the middle of all the trees he saw his first Christmas crib. While Mary smiled at the Infant Jesus, Joseph and the shepherds stood watching.

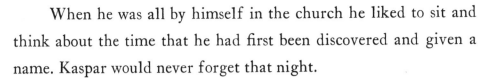

He had wanted to get a better look at the Baby so he climbed to the edge of the manger. But the smell of the firs made him very, very drowsy, and Kaspar fell fast asleep.

The next thing he knew a young man was bending over him.

"Ach, du kleine Maus. Ah, you little mouse," he said softly. "I shall call you 'Kleinmaus. Little Mouse.'"

He spoke so kindly that Kaspar didn't want to run away.

"And since, like the Wise Men, you have come to visit the Christ Child, I shall call you 'Kaspar,' after one of them." The young man half-whispered, "Kaspar Kleinmaus," as he stroked his velvety fur.

"What a beautiful name!" thought Kaspar, and he looked thankfully at his new friend.

He soon saw that the whole village loved this young pastor, Father Joseph Mohr. The old ladies knitted socks for him, the middle-aged ladies baked cakes for him, and the young ladies sang for him. To the men he was both a friend and a brother. They came to him when they needed advice about buying a farm, building a house, or playing chess. And the children thought of him as a second father who helped with their lessons and shared in their games.

Kaspar soon found out that Father Mohr loved to sing. Since Kaspar never grew tired of listening, he went to every church service.

"I don't know why I love the music so," Kaspar often said to himself. "I don't know why, I just do."

Kaspar was sure that no choir in the whole world sang as sweetly as theirs. He listened even when they practiced. Sometimes he tried to sing along with them.

He thought that the choirmaster, Mr. Franz Gruber, was a good organist. Who else could bring such beautiful music from that weak old organ?

Mr. Gruber was rather stout so Kaspar could tell he enjoyed eating. This interested Kaspar, who was not stout, but liked to eat, too.

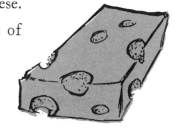

The pockets of Mr. Gruber's coat were always bulging with goodies his wife had given him. He munched constantly while he practiced the organ. Sometimes he brought only bread and cheese. But other times he had a slice of fresh gingerbread or a piece of sugary coffeecake.

Mr. Gruber would place his tidbit on the edge of the organ and take a bite now and then. Kaspar waited anxiously for these moments and caught all the crumbs that missed Mr. Gruber's mouth.

He enjoyed licking up the sticky raisins hour after hour, but chasing the cherries and nuts across the floor was the real fun. And when the organist was in a hurry, he often dashed away forgetting his half-eaten goody. Kaspar ate all that was left.

During such feasts he sighed deeply, "There is indeed great joy in being a church mouse. Great joy!"

All went well in Kaspar's life until one day when Mr. Gruber noticed a small hole in the floor. Father Mohr happened to be in church.

"What's that?" asked Mr. Gruber suspiciously. "I didn't know that we had mice in our church." The tone of his voice made Kaspar tremble in his hiding place.

Kaspar heard Father Mohr's gentle tones, "Yes, yes, Franz, you are both right and wrong. St. Nicholas' has not mice. It has *a* mouse."

"Just one! That's fine," answered Mr. Gruber. "It can be caught very easily."

"Ach, nein! Oh, no!" replied the priest quickly. "I—I couldn't catch him."

"Of course not, no one would expect you to. But the traps nowadays are excellent," said Mr. Gruber encouragingly.

Kaspar shivered with fear and every hair of his fur coat stood on end.

"Franz, I know full well that a fine church such as St. Nicholas' should have a cat instead of a mouse," continued Father Mohr, "but, when one has seen a wee creature practically born before one's eyes, one feels . . ."

"A mouse born right here in our church!" gasped Mr. Gruber. "My, we do need a cat!"

"Well, I had noticed a mouse," stated Father Mohr firmly, "when I first came to St. Nicholas'. Perhaps it was his father or mother. Anyway it disappeared."

"Then where did this fellow come from?" asked the organist.

Kaspar listened quietly as he heard the pastor tell how he had found him in the Christmas crib.

Mr. Gruber's face changed as he said, "No wonder you feel the way you do about him, Father. But why don't you take him home with you?"

"To the rectory? Oh, no! My housekeeper hates mice," replied the priest sadly.

"That's too bad, but I really don't believe the church is the proper place for him, do you?"

"Maybe not," answered Father Mohr. "But there is absolutely nothing I can do about it. He will have to stay here."

How happy Kaspar was to hear that he could keep his own home—the only one he had ever known—and that Father Mohr wanted him to stay.

Now the winter holidays had come again. Kaspar was excited just thinking about all the wonderful cookies and cakes and candies. But so far he hadn't even got a sniff. The baking was popped right out of the ovens and into tin boxes. Everything was being saved for Christmas Day.

And Mr. Gruber seldom came to practice, because the old organ needed fixing. Kaspar's mouth watered, as he thought of the good food that he was missing. "Oh, how I wish I had some of Mrs. Gruber's gingerbread!"

The more that Kaspar thought about eating, the more his poor little stomach ached with hunger.

"I've never been so empty," he groaned. "I can't wait any longer. I must eat something. And I'm going to do it right away."

He looked around the church. Then he sat quietly thinking for a while.

Kaspar looked around the church again. When his eyes rested on the organ he remembered a wonderful story his mother had told him about his grandmother. Many years ago this good mouse had lived for two whole weeks on a pair of leather shoe laces.

"Whoop-ee," he half-shouted, "the organ bellows are leather. I'll eat them. The organ doesn't work well anyway, so I'm sure no one will care. Besides Mr. Gruber doesn't like me. It was he who suggested a mousetrap!"

Opening his mouth as wide as he could, Kaspar took a great big bite of the bellows.

"My, this thing is tough. Worse than the oldest cheese. I only hope I don't break a tooth," he mumbled to himself.

He couldn't help but feel that the choir would be glad to find the organ would not play. "No more false notes," he kept repeating, "no more false notes to ruin their lovely songs."

As he nibbled away Kaspar thought again of his mother. He had been told that he looked like her. He could still see her soft brown eyes and her dark gray fur. She had come from beautiful Vienna in a bag of corn. She often talked about the tasty foods that had made her city famous.

Kaspar's father, big and strong, had been born in the lovely town of Salzburg close by. And his black beady eyes simply danced when he told of the housewives' treasured recipes.

And now their son, who had inherited their keen appetite for fine foods, must dine on the dried-out bellows of an organ.

"Ah, well, that's that," sighed Kaspar, as he ambled down the aisle. Climbing into a pew, he huddled in a dark corner for his nap.

Before Kaspar could sleep in came Mr. Gruber. Naturally he had to practice for the Christmas Eve service. He sat down quietly at the organ and started to play.

"Ach, Himmel! Oh, Heavens!" he moaned. "Just listen. Now it doesn't work at all."

There were tears in his voice, and he kept running his hands back and forth through his hair. "What shall we do? All our beautiful hymns! If only the organ had lasted for Midnight Mass!"

Then bending over quickly he examined the organ. Kaspar watched him closely. "Just as I thought. Just as I thought," shouted Mr. Gruber angrily. "That mouse again! Drat it! I'll tell Father Mohr!" And out he rushed.

"Oh, dear," murmured Kaspar sleepily, "and I had thought I was doing the choir a favor. I only meant to help."

Surely only Mr. Gruber would feel this way. Why should he be so upset, Kaspar wondered. The old organ didn't work properly anyway. Besides, it wasn't as if the organist had no musical instrument at all! Kaspar had overheard the choir girls teasing Mr. Gruber about his guitar. They claimed that he really liked it better than the organ and spent all his free time composing guitar music.

But Kaspar had not meant to make Mr. Gruber so very angry.
To make himself feel better he thought of all the good things that
he had done for St. Nicholas'.

He was doing his duty by keeping the floors neat and tidy. He
cleaned up all crumbs and bits of paper. Never was there an ant or
a bug. Certainly no village church in all Austria could possibly be
as well cared for as St. Nicholas'. With a clear conscience Kaspar
curled up again and finished his nap.

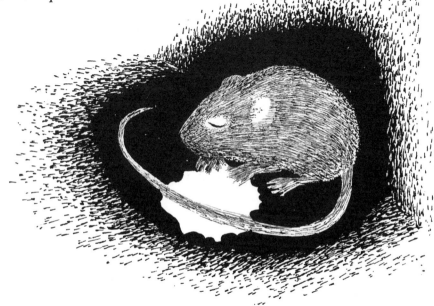

Kaspar slept and slept; just how long he didn't know. He was awakened by the sound of creaking door hinges and footsteps. Jumping up with a start, he found it had grown very, very dark outside.

He looked around him. Kaspar saw Father Mohr kneeling before the dimly lit altar. The priest had on an overcoat and held his hat by his side. He was praying out loud. Kaspar slipped down quietly and tiptoed closer, because he wanted to listen.

This is what Kaspar heard:

> Silent Night, Holy Night!
> All is calm, all is bright,
> Round yon Virgin Mother and Child,
> Holy Infant so tender and mild;
> Sleep in heavenly peace,
> Sleep in heavenly peace.

Kaspar knew that Father Mohr always knelt alone and prayed for the sick of his parish. Yet somehow this "Silent Night, Holy Night" did not sound like a prayer to Kaspar.

Kaspar was curious. Why was the priest here at this hour? And why was he dressed to go out?

Kaspar made up his mind to follow Father Mohr. He would solve the mystery for himself.

As soon as Father Mohr left the church Kaspar left, too. The night was cold and bright with stars. The priest walked briskly and Kaspar frolicked behind him in the moonlight. Before long Kaspar realized they were on the road to Arnsdorf, only two miles away.

Kaspar knew Arnsdorf well, because it was the home of Franz Gruber, organist, choirmaster, and village schoolteacher. He was one of Father Mohr's best friends.

Kaspar's heart was gay. As he skipped along he made up his mind that he would never leave this beautiful countryside.

He loved it all year round. He loved it in the winter with snow and more snow, warm porcelain stoves, and sugar cookies. And in the spring with soft green moss, sunshine, bird calls, and cool streams. And in the summer with wheat fields sprinkled with poppies, cornflowers, butterflies, and with picnics. And in the fall with nut hunting and windy romps among the colored leaves. Who could ask for more?

Kaspar woke from his daydreaming when Father Mohr came to a quick stop.

He almost bumped into him. Kaspar saw that they had already reached the Grubers' house. While waiting for someone to answer the door they both stomped the snow from their feet.

Mr. Gruber opened the door. "Father Mohr, how happy we are to see you! Please, come right in." The priest stepped inside.

Kaspar followed quickly. He was so quiet no one noticed him. Father Mohr said, "I apologize for this late hour. I realize it is past midnight. I do hope I am not disturbing anyone, but I very much wanted to read you something."

"Fine, fine. You know we are always delighted to see you. Do make yourself comfortable. Come, Elisabeth, come," called Mr. Gruber as he walked toward the kitchen. "Father Mohr is here!"

Mrs. Gruber appeared, surrounded by a very large apron. "How nice to see you, Father. Now don't worry about disturbing the children for they have been asleep hours. The day before Christmas we get little sleep. I'm still putting cookies into the oven."

"Oven!" The word stuck in Kaspar's mind. The thought of Mrs. Gruber's baking made him forget the purpose of his trip. For a moment he stood still. Then as he sniffed the air his whiskers danced with glee. The house was fragrant with delicious odors of sugary cake dough, so he skipped gaily into the kitchen.

Mrs. Gruber had not had time to sweep the floor. Kaspar squeaked for joy. Cookie crumbs were everywhere. Peppernuts, sand tarts, springerle, cinnamon stars, and almond cookies! Appointing himself to collect the crumbs, Kaspar dashed busily here and there. This was the tastiest and easiest cleaning job that he had ever done.

Kaspar did not dare linger long in the kitchen. He tiptoed carefully into the front room and hid behind the big porcelain stove where he warmed his tiny body and toasted his toes.

He found Father Mohr had not removed his coat and was insisting that he could not stay. The Grubers were excited. Kaspar thought Father Mohr looked unusually pleased.

"Really, Father, I think your words are beautiful. They sing themselves. 'Stille Nacht, Heilige Nacht. Silent Night, Holy Night,'" repeated Mr. Gruber.

"I think they are lovely, too," added Mrs. Gruber.

"Oh, thank you very, very much. I had hoped that you would like them," said Father Mohr modestly.

"I certainly do, and I'll start working on your idea right away," answered the organist.

"Franz, you know how sorry I am about the organ. Perhaps you'll accept this poem as a Christmas thought?"

"How kind of you, Father! Indeed, I am honored. But, please, stop worrying. You had no way of knowing that the mouse would chew the bellows," replied Mr. Gruber.

"Thank you," said the priest. "Since tonight is our big celebration I must be going."

"Good-by, Father. We'll see you at Midnight Mass."

"Auf Wiedersehen, and God bless you," called Father Mohr.

Off they went again, but this time they were on their way home. Kaspar still did not understand about this "Silent Night, Holy Night" that Father Mohr kept repeating.

Now he was too weary to care. Nor did he worry about this mysterious visit late into the night, for he had never had such fun. His stomach was delightfully filled with Christmas cookies.

Kaspar really was very, very tired from this long excursion. He was sure Father Mohr's housekeeper wouldn't be awake, so he decided to spend the rest of the night with Father Mohr in his warm little house.

At last, Oberndorf was right in front of them. Kaspar was glad!

By the time Father Mohr had blown his light out, Kaspar was already sound asleep. He was cozily cuddled in Father Mohr's woolen socks right under the bed dreaming of Christmas.

When Kaspar awoke, he found the day perfect—crisp and clear with the snow crunching underfoot.

As evening approached, the big bell in the tower of St. Nicholas' seemed to toll louder and longer than ever before. Kaspar stood watching the crowds with their lanterns as they hurried to church in their holiday clothes— girls in dirndl dresses with flowered scarfs, boys in Tyrolean jackets and leather breeches, women in flowing dresses, and men in their Sunday suits and hats.

The tall stained-glass windows seemed to beckon to Kaspar with their long colored shadows across the glistening snow. Yet for the first time in his life he hesitated attending Midnight Mass. But he could not stay away. St. Nicholas' was his home.

Kaspar only hoped that Father Mohr was not too worried about the organ and that Mr. Gruber had forgiven him.

Until he reached the church door he had forgotten how truly beautiful St. Nicholas' could be at Christmas time. Many, many candles were burning upon the high altar. And the church was decorated with evergreens and boughs of pine.

Although the service had not begun, all the pews were filled to overflowing. As Kaspar gazed at the Christmas crib, Father Mohr and the altar boys entered.

When the priest announced that the organ was out of order, Kaspar heard hushed whisperings everywhere. And he noticed the people looked sad.

Kaspar had hoped that the choir might be pleased. But now he knew they were just as disappointed as Mr. Gruber. He had never felt so unhappy. Since the whole congregation missed their organ this was no "Merry Christmas" for Kaspar.

"Yes," he decided, "I'd better leave town as soon as the service is over. They'll be sure to get a cat now."

Once again he tried to remember his mother's words of wisdom. After all, she had left Vienna. Maybe he could travel in a bag of corn and go elsewhere, too. It certainly wouldn't be much fun being all alone. Maybe he could locate a distant cousin in nearby Salzburg.

Just when Kaspar was his unhappiest he noticed Mr. Gruber had picked up his guitar. To Kaspar's surprise the organist began to play and sing. His mellow voice floated down from the choir loft, filling the church. Father Mohr joined him in the song. Right away Kaspar recognized the words:

ROUND YON VIR - GIN MOTH-ER AND CHILD.
Nur das trau-te, hoch-hei-li-ge Paar.

HO - LY IN-FANT SO TEN-DER AND MILD,
Hol-der kna-be im lok-ki-gen Haar,

SLEEP IN HEAV-EN-LY PEACE, —
Schlaf' in himm-li-scher Ruh', —

SLEEP IN HEAV-EN-LY PEACE.
Schlaf' in himm-li-scher Ruh'.

The faces of the people lighted up, and the priest's eyes were filled with tears. During his whole life Kaspar had never heard such a lovely song. It was perfect.

As the choir girls sang the refrain, "Sleep in heavenly peace," Kaspar felt as if he were present in the stable that first Christmas Night. "How wonderful it would be to hear this beautiful song again next year!" thought Kaspar.

But, alas, he would be gone next Christmas. The people would still remember that he had hurt their organ.

Finally Midnight Mass was over. By hurrying, Kaspar was the first one down the aisle. He hid behind the church door right near the baptismal font as the people swarmed toward the entrance. He could hear the congregation talking about the new hymn.

Everyone was asking questions at once. "What was the name of that beautiful song?" "Why haven't we heard it before?" "Where did it come from?" "Who wrote it?" "The words?" "The music?"

Luckily Mr. Gruber soon appeared from the choir loft, and he told the simple story.

In the early hours of that very morning Father Mohr had written about their little village of Oberndorf sleeping so peacefully. The holy quietness of Christmastide seemed to fill every home, great and small, rich and poor, just as it had done in the little town of Bethlehem once long, long ago.

Before dawn Father Mohr had trudged through the snow to bring these words to Franz Gruber. The organist had been inspired and immediately composed all the music. Since a mouse had damaged the organ bellows he had decided to play the melody on his guitar. The choir had rehearsed the song, so the congregation would not be disappointed on Christmas Eve.

All the people were wild with joy—grownups and children, too! This new Christmas hymn was played for the first time in their very own church. How wonderful! The words of their own dear priest, Father Joseph Mohr! And the music of their own organist, Franz Gruber!

"Merry Christmas, Merry Christmas everybody," called the happy crowd as they started to hurry home. But Kaspar felt lonely. Just then someone remarked, "Now don't forget, if there hadn't been holes in the bellows we'd have heard the same old organ and the same Christmas songs."

"Maybe you're right," laughed Mr. Gruber. "Here's thanks to the mouse!"

Kaspar could hardly believe his ears. Suddenly everyone was pleased, so Kaspar was happy again. Even Mr. Gruber was no longer angry with him! Chills of joy ran up his tiny spine.

Now Kaspar knew that he would not have to leave his home. He knew, too, that St. Nicholas' would never get a mousetrap or a cat.

Amid the laughter and jolly greetings that floated down the church steps and out into the village square Kaspar heard, "A Merry Christmas to the mouse! A Merry Christmas to our church mouse!"

The children ran everywhere searching and calling, "Where is the little mouse? Where is the little mouse?"

But Kaspar Kleinmaus was nowhere to be found. Giving a big
squeak, he had scampered back to take one more bite of the bellows.